little miss Wise

by Roger Hargreaves

Little Miss Wise was as wise as an owl.

Possibly two owls.

Being so wise and sensible meant
that Little Miss Wise
brushed her teeth every day,
made her bed every day,
tidied her house every day,
and did lots of other
wise and sensible things.

If you are as wise as Little Miss Wise,
you'll know just what kind of other things she did.

Little Miss Wise liked to go for a walk
every day.

A walk that was neither too long, nor too short.

A walk that was wise and sensible.

Or sensible and wise, if you prefer.

On her walks she often met other people.

People who were not quite so wise.

And sometimes, people who were decidely unwise.

Last Monday she met Little Miss Naughty.

"Come and jump in the puddles!"
cried Little Miss Naughty,
with a naughty gleam in her eye.

But Little Miss Wise,
being wise,
refused.

She didn't want to get HER feet wet.

On Tuesday she met Little Miss Greedy,
who was carrying an enormous cake filled
with cream and smothered with pink icing.

"Would you like some of this?"
asked Little Miss Greedy.

Little Miss Wise refused.

She didn't want an upset stomach.

On Wednesday Little Miss Wise refused
to get into Mr Busy's racing car.

She didn't want to have an accident.

On Thursday she refused to go into
Mr Messy's house.

"If I go into his house I will get dirty,"
she said to herself.

But she didn't say anything to Mr Messy.

She didn't want to hurt his feelings.

On Friday she refused to
play tennis with Mr Silly.

There's nothing silly about that,
is there?

By Saturday, Little Miss Wise was feeling unhappy.

"If I keep saying 'no' all the time, I'll upset everybody and I won't have any friends left," she said to herself.

She thought long and hard about the problem, and being the wise and sensible person she is, she came up with an answer.

"From now on, I will say 'yes' to everything."

On Sunday, while she was out on one of her
wise and sensible walks, or sensible and wise
walks, if you prefer, Little Miss Wise met Mr Mischief.

He was carrying a parcel.

"Please accept this small present," he said to her.

"N..." began Little Miss Wise.
but then she remembered her decision.

"Yes! Thank you!" she cried.

She took the parcel.

And off skipped Mr Mischief
with a mischievous grin on his face.

Little Miss Wise opened the parcel.

"ATISHOO!" she sneezed.

Then she sneezed again.

And she sneezed, and sneezed, and sneezed
all day long.

She used 199 handkerchiefs.

Mr Mischief's present
had been sneezing powder!

Today is Monday and Little Miss Wise
has stopped sneezing.

She is on one of her wise and sensible walks,
or sensible and wise walks, if you prefer,
and she has met Mr Nonsense.

"Would you like to ride in my aeroplane?" he asks.

"N..." Little Miss Wise starts to say.

But then she changes her mind and exclaims:
"Oh, yes please!"

You think she is being very unwise, don't you?
You think she should have learnt her
lesson by now, don't you?

Well she is safe this time.

Because Mr Nonsense's aeroplane
doesn't have any wings,
or an engine,
or even wheels.

It's just a doormat.

Have you ever heard of such nonsense!

Fantastic offers for Little Miss fans!

**Collect all your Mr. Men or
Little Miss books in these superb
durable collectors' cases!**
Only £5.99 inc. postage and packing,
these wipe-clean, hard-wearing cases
will give all your Mr. Men or Little Miss
books a beautiful new home!

**Keep track of your collection with
this giant-sized double-sided Mr. Men
and Little Miss Collectors' poster.**
Collect 6 tokens and we will send you a
brilliant giant-sized double-sided collectors'
poster! Simply tape a £1 coin to
cover postage and
packing in the
space provided
and fill out the
form overleaf.

**STICK
£1 COIN
HERE**
(for poster
only)

Only need a few Little Miss or Mr. Men to complete your set? You can order any of the titles on the back of the books from our Mr. Men order line on 0870 787 1724. Orders should be delivered between 5 and 7 working days.

--- **TO BE COMPLETED BY AN ADULT** ---

To apply for any of these great offers, ask an adult to complete the details below and send this whole page with the appropriate payment and tokens, to: MR. MEN CLASSIC OFFER, PO BOX 715, HORSHAM RH12 5WG

☐ Please send me a giant-sized double-sided collectors' poster.
AND ☐ I enclose 6 tokens and have taped a £1 coin to the other side of this page.

☐ Please send me ☐ Mr. Men Library case(s) and/or ☐ Little Miss library case(s) at £5.99 each inc P&P

☐ I enclose a cheque/postal order payable to Egmont UK Limited for £................

OR ☐ Please debit my MasterCard / Visa / Maestro / Delta account (delete as appropriate) for £................

Card no. ☐☐☐☐☐☐☐☐☐☐☐☐☐☐☐☐☐☐☐ Security code ☐☐☐

Issue no. (if available) ☐ Start Date ☐☐/☐☐/☐☐ Expiry Date ☐☐/☐☐/☐☐

Fan's name: .... Date of birth: ....

Address: ....

....

.... Postcode: ....

Name of parent / guardian: ....

Email for parent / guardian: ....

Signature of parent / guardian: ....

Please allow 28 days for delivery. Offer is only available while stocks last. We reserve the right to change the terms of this offer at any time and we offer a 14 day money back guarantee. This does not affect your statutory rights. Offers apply to UK only.

☐ We may occasionally wish to send you information about other Egmont children's books.
If you would rather we didn't, please tick this box.

Ref: LIM 001